BEFORE, THEN, NOW

S. E. GREEN

Copyright © S. E. Green, 2024

The right of S. E. Green to be identified as the author of this work has been asserted per the Copyright, Designs and Patents Act 1976. All rights reserved. No part of this publication may be reproduced, transmitted, or stored in a retrieval system, in any form or by any means, without permission in writing from the publisher, nor be otherwise circulated in any form of binding or cover other than that in which it is published and without a similar condition being imposed on the subsequent purchaser. All characters in this publication are fictitious and any resemblance to real people, alive or dead, is purely coincidental.

1

Current Day

*C*oma.

That's what I'm in. But I don't know how that can be so.

I can hear—hushed voices, beeping machines.

I can smell—antiseptic, mild perfume.

I can feel—the needle in my left arm, chilled fingers on my face.

I know who I am—Benjamin (Benny) Thorton, twenty-one, college student.

But I can't speak. Or move. Or see. Believe me, I've tried all three. I've tried to separate my lips. To pry my eyelids open. To make my vocal cords vibrate. Yet nothing happens.

I've been this way for twelve hours. At least that's what the people in my room say.

Coma.

Someone just said that word again.

How long does a coma last? In some instances, maybe years, right? I don't know.

Sounds of multiple shoes move across the bare floor, one squeaking and the other a soft tread. The door opens, then closes.

Silence.

Someone breathes out. *Mom, is that you?* I wait for her to speak, to touch me, but nothing happens.

I dig around in my brain, searching, pleading for clarity. How am I here? What's the last thing I remember? I recall going to my girlfriend Shauna's dorm. We needed to talk. I received a text from my best friend Dean: I'M SORRY. I remember Mom's face when I—

"Benny?" a young female speaks. Her voice is melodic and familiar, yet I can't place it. "Don't die. Please don't die."

~

WHEN I WAS SEVENTEEN, I almost cut the tip of my index finger off. It stayed attached, just barely. It happened while I was trimming the bushes at my house with an electric trimmer. For a brief second I looked away, and there my finger went. There was so much blood, but oddly no pain.

With my finger wrapped in a towel, I drove myself to the emergency room. They ushered me back, and that was when the pain started. Perhaps the adrenaline of the moment kept me focused and agony free, but once it began, my God, was it excruciating.

Do you know how many nerve endings exist in a fingertip? Three thousand. I looked it up.

The doctor gave me a shot in the finger to numb it so that she could sew things back together. The shot hurt worse than the pain. I yelled "FUCK!" so loudly that two doctors and three nurses came running.

I say all of this because I have never felt pain like that since, until now.

"FUCK!" I try yelling that word but nothing comes out. Instead, it sticks inside of me, bouncing around like a pinball.

Unlike my finger where the pain radiated outward, this agony radiates inward. Everywhere. I don't know what happened to cause my body so much suffering. I'd ask but my lips won't move. They're so wide open my jaw hurts with the object—I assume is a ventilator—pushing its way inside my body.

"Oh my goodness," a raspy female voice says. "How horrible. What happened to him?"

"Not sure yet," another female voice answers, this one older. "I just got here. His name is Benjamin."

"Benjamin," the raspy one says, moving closer to me, "my shift just started. I'm going to take good care of you." She touches my hand and inwardly I flinch. Hers is ice cold.

The two women move around the room. One set of hands coasts over me, checking my body here and there. I wish they'd talk some more. I want to know what's wrong with me.

"There," the older one says. "That should make you feel better."

Oh, she's right. That does make me feel better. Warmth flows through my veins. I sink into it, relishing relief it offers. My head feels fuzzy. If I could, I'd smile and thank her. Even though I'm lying down, my body sways. I don't know what she gave me, but I want more of it. I no longer feel pain.

"Any family?" the raspy one asks.

"Not sure. I'll have to check the visitation log."

The door opens. A male voice says, "Shauna Sandford is here. She's his wife."

My wife?

"We're just finishing up," the older nurse says. "She can come on in."

Female voices curl through the air, floating around inside my head. They merge with the fuzziness, trying to form a semblance of words and sentences, but not quite clicking. I focus hard, eventually giving up and drifting toward the oblivion of the medicine.

Some time later I drift back, only slightly experiencing the pain from earlier. Someone coughs. Then he, or she, releases a heavy sigh.

"They say you can hear me," Shauna speaks. "I... don't know what to say."

She moves closer. Her hair touches my cheek. I think she's going to kiss me, but she doesn't. I smell her breath. It doesn't smell good. That's the one thing about Shauna that I don't adore—her breath oftentimes borders halitosis. One time I delicately pointed it out, and she didn't talk to me for nearly a week.

Shauna doesn't move. What is she doing? Why is she leaning over me like that? She sighs again. It sounds loud. I wish I could pinch my nostrils to block out her breath.

Then a sudden realization moves through me, circulating, building, filling me with anger.

I'm mad at my wife, yet I have no clue why.

2

A Few Days Ago

I stare at the unmoving ceiling fan, listening to my sound machine, willing my alarm to go off. Last I looked I still had ten minutes. Under the weighted blanket, I roll over, curling around the body pillow that's supposed to help me sleep.

Rain patters my windows, as it's been doing all night. With the hurricane circling in the Atlantic, we're supposed to get this for days to come.

Oh, joy.

I consider getting up, but no matter how quiet I am, somehow my mom knows. Then she'll worry I'm not sleeping—which I'm not, but that's not the point. The point is she'll buy me yet one more thing that never works for my chronic insomnia.

Yeah, I've done it all. Hypnosis tracks. Brown noise.

White noise. Black noise. Pills. Counting sheep. Breathing exercises. Journaling. Hot bath. Herbal remedies. THC.

Nothing brings me sleep.

It could be worse.

On the nightstand rests my phone, plugged in and charging. I power it up. Across the room, an air dispenser releases a squirt of lavender—yet another thing that's supposed to help.

My phone lights up with a text from Shauna that came in late last night.

Shauna: CAN'T DO LUNCH, SORRY.

Shauna's been canceling on me a lot lately. I text her back a thumbs up, trying not to take it personally. I don't want to be "that" boyfriend.

My alarm chirps. *Finally.*

In the bathroom, I turn the shower on. While I wait for it to heat up, I brush my teeth and survey myself in the mirror.

I look bad.

With bloodshot eyes, lifeless skin, and stooped shoulders, I look every bit the insomniac that I am. What I'd give for several hours of uninterrupted sleep.

Instead, I pop a couple of caffeine pills. I can't afford to fall asleep in class.

Shower and shave behind me, Visine, and with pomade in my short dark hair, I pass by Mom's room, finding it empty with the same freshly-laundered clothes hanging on her closet door that have been there for two days. I locate her in the living room, stretched out on the couch watching TV.

I force my eyes alert and tall body upright. I even put a chirp to my voice. "Good morning!"

Still dressed in yesterday's clothes, she smiles. "Don't you look rested."

"Must be the new addition to my room. Thank you for the lavender."

"You're very welcome."

"How about eggs for breakfast?" I ask, wishing instead I had a Red Bull and apple fritter.

"I was hoping you'd say that. I'm in the mood for eggs as well." She goes back to her show and I move to the kitchen, prepping coffee and putting a skillet on the range.

I note a grocery list pinned beneath a magnet on the refrigerator. It's been there for a few days. Guess I'd better get it taken care of. I remove it and place it in my pocket, telling her, "I'll tackle groceries later."

"Aren't you sweet? Thank you. You know I have a lot going on today."

Translation: She'll put on that outfit hanging on her closet door, and then spend an hour opening the front door, then closing it. Opening, then closing. Opening, then closing. Hell, she may even make it out to the front porch, but not likely. The one highlight of her day will be an Amazon delivery.

I wish she'd enroll in grocery service, but she doesn't like the way they "pick out produce."

I serve Mom scrambled eggs and we eat together, watching the morning news. Mom's green station wagon sits in the same spot as always in the driveway with my well-used old Toyota behind it. I always fear it won't start, but it does every time.

I take my time driving to campus.

I graduate in a few months with a degree in finance. I don't know what I'm going to do. There are only so many jobs in my small hometown of Saint Augustine, Florida. I can't live with Mom forever, but every time I broach the subject, she launches into a full-on panic attack.

Like last night. I told her I want to propose to Shauna, and before I got much else out she started crying and begging me not to leave her. So, I promised I wouldn't. It's what I always do. My whole life centers around Mom's mental well-being.

I cruise through Dunkin Donuts, get that apple fritter, make a stop at CVS for more caffeine pills, and then drive the rest of the way to campus. I park under the only palm tree fat enough to provide shade.

September heat snakes around me as I eat the fritter and walk toward the business school. Off to the right sits the education building with its attached preschool. Most of Shauna's classes are in there. For a woman who doesn't particularly like children, I've always found it odd that she's an education major. She says it's apples and oranges. *You don't have to like kids to teach them.* Doesn't make sense to me, but who am I to question her reasoning? I don't like numbers and I'm in finance—job security and all that.

Soothing air conditioning coats my skin as I walk through the business school's lobby. I cut off to where a coffee cart sits and throw away the bag my apple fritter came in.

"Hey, Benny. Usual?" the coffee cart girl greets me in her usual bright and cheery voice.

I nod, wishing for the zillionth time that I knew her name. But we're way past that period where I can innocently ask, *Remind me what your name is?*

With my Red Eye drink—a regular hot coffee with an added shot of espresso—in hand, I slowly take the stairs up to the second floor. As I do, I sip my beverage, loving how it cuts the sugar of the fritter. I pause and glance idly out the wall of windows that overlook the education building and the campus beyond. I'm not sure why I stop. It's certainly not in hopes I'll get a glimpse of Shauna. Her first class comes later in the morning.

No, I stop because an awareness buzzes along my skin. Something's not right. From my vantage point on the stairwell, I peer out the wall of windows, my gaze carefully roaming over others moving across campus, students entering and exiting buildings, cars pulling in and out of lots...

I freeze.

There, in a small park on the other side of the education building, stands my mom staring at me.

"Benny?"

I jerk around, finding the coffee cart girl. With a smile, she hands me my credit card. "You left this." I take it from her and am about to turn back to the windows when she says, "Um, I'm not sure if you're still dating Shauna or not, but—"

"I am. Yes." I hold up the credit card. "Thanks for this."

"Oh...sure." She backs away with an embarrassed smile. "See you around, I guess."

I turn back to the windows. But Mom is gone.

3
———

Childhood

Cross-legged I sit on the floor of my bedroom, staring at the TV dinner I ate and licked clean, listening to Dad yell and to Mom cry.

It's like this every night.

Sometimes things get thrown, but I've never seen him hit her. Not that that makes a difference. His words do as much damage. I don't know why Mom stays with him. He's an asshole. I wish he'd move on to the part of the evening where he drinks himself into a stupor.

Yeah, my parents are nothing like my only friend, Dean's. Mine don't laugh and talk, and they never say *I love you* to each other.

I wish Dean's parents would adopt me, but then who would watch out for Mom? I always worry about her, but she seems so fine in the morning as she makes small talk and occasionally cooks me breakfast, which in my house means oatmeal in the microwave.

There's this kid at school whose parents frequently leave him home alone. I envy that kid. I'd give anything to be alone and not hear this every night.

A siren echoes in the distance. I bet a neighbor called the cops. It wouldn't be the first time.

An object hits the other side of my wall, the one that butts up to my parents' room. It doesn't faze me.

There's a loud banging on our front door. With a sigh, I get to my feet and go to let the cops in. Maybe I'll get lucky and this will be one of the nights they haul Dad off. Now and again that happens, and it's the only night I get solid sleep.

No such luck.

After the cops leave, I crawl out my window and walk to Dean's house.

Dean and his parents left on vacation. I stood there earlier, observing as they excitedly planned the trip to Carlsbad Caverns, hoping beyond the universe that they would invite me to join them.

They didn't.

My family never goes on vacation. Even if my parents decided to do one, I wouldn't want to be a part of it. It would be more of the same old thing. No thank you.

One whole week. That's how long Dean and his parents will be gone and I'll be here in their house, enjoying my own vacation.

Do I have a spare key? Of course not. But I know where they keep it—in a fake piece of poop hidden under an oleander bush.

Will my parents know I'm gone? That's laughable.

It only takes me five minutes. I find the fake poop and the key and make myself comfortable on Dean's bed. I toast the air with my middle finger.

Happy fuckin' tenth birthday to me.

4

Current Day

Long fingers with unkempt nails reach for me. The moon glints off of the nearly translucent skin as they emerge through the darkness. The hands draw closer. And closer...

My still body lifts and floats, at first, as if invisible strings hold me in place. The strings snap. I fall fast, plummeting toward earth. Shades of dark streak pass. I scream so loudly that my throat hurts. My body hurtles toward the ground.

I jerk awake. My heart races. I won't be going back to sleep, not after that. I try to get out of bed, but I'm stuck in a different nightmare where a coma has rendered me mute and paralyzed. Because that's the word a man is currently saying. *Paralyzed.*

"We won't know for sure until, or if, he wakes, but there is a good chance he will be paralyzed."

Silence.

A clearing throat.

"What is the chance he won't wake?" Shauna asks.

"It's too soon to tell. It's not even been twenty-four hours yet," the man, who I assume is a doctor, responds. "He fell six stories. His injuries are significant. Internal bleeding, broken bones, cracked skull, fractured spine, bruises..."

I fell six stories? That's impossible. I live in a historical town where building codes prohibit anything taller than three stories. There are no six-story buildings.

Wait, that's not true. There is one building six stories tall that was built before the codes were created. It's one of the oldest structures in our town. Shauna lives in that building.

Buzz.

"Do you need to get that?" the doctor asks.

"No," Shauna replies.

"Has your husband been sad lately?" the doctor asks next.

Silence. Then, "Um, a little upset, yes."

I have?

"How long have you been married?" the doctor asks.

"Not long. It's brand new."

Buzz.

"You can get that if you need to," the doctor insists.

"It's fine," Shauna tells him.

"How did you get that black eye?" the doctor asks.

Shauna has a black eye?

"I fell. I know how that sounds, but I really did."

"Okay," the doctor replies.

Buzz.

"Do you need anything?" the doctor asks.

"No, I'm fine."

"Hang in there." The doctor's shoes make a suction

sound as he walks from the room. The door opens, then closes.

Tap-tap-tapping fills the quiet space. That's Shauna's phone. A faint ring filters from the speaker, followed by a muffled voice.

Shauna snaps, "I told you to stop texting me." She listens to whoever is on the other end. "No, I haven't done it yet. Given what's happened, I haven't had time."

More muffled words.

"Yes, I blame you. Benny would never have been on that roof if it wasn't for your big mouth."

She clicks off. Heavy, irritated breaths fill the space. I sense her move closer to me. Her voice comes low and unsteady. "Whichever way this situation ends up, I'm definitely going through with it."

Her words leave me feeling as if I'm frozen in time with a person I never knew.

~

DEAN IS HERE.

There's not a childhood memory I have that doesn't involve him. We met in preschool, or rather our moms met, and the playdates began. Our mothers didn't click, but they knew how much we liked each other and continued scheduling the playdates for us.

Things were always difficult at my house. Thankfully, I spent a lot of time at Dean's place. His mom became my mom as my own quietly and gradually withdrew. I worked hard to keep the peace. I never once wanted my mom to think I'd chosen Dean's mother over her.

Filled with unusual nervous energy, Dean now paces my

hospital room. With each pass by my bed, his cologne drifts over me.

Beyond the walls and windows of the hospital, wind whistles. It's the kind of Florida wind generated solely during hurricane season. Mom hates wind like this. I don't blame her. Our house isn't the most stable structure. Even a slight breeze sometimes creaks the roof. I think of the palm tree in our side yard with the fronds touching the gutter. I meant to trim that. In weather like this, it sounds like long, gnarly fingernails scraping metal.

Outside, a gust swirls. Something hits the window. Inside, I flinch, suddenly no longer here.

I'm standing on the roof of Shauna's building. It's night. Overhead, storm clouds move in. Dust lifts from the rooftop, spiraling around me, slow at first, then picking up pace. Long brown hair whips my cheek. My feet inch closer to the roof's edge. The dust whirling around me dissipates. The storm clouds shift, allowing the moon to make an appearance. It illuminates the area, growing brighter, spotlighting the ground six stories below where I now lay, my body mangled. A shadow glides close to my unmoving heap of bones, meat, and organs. The wind picks up again, sending the distinct smell of cologne up my nostrils.

And I'm back here, heavy on the hospital bed, listening to Dean pace and smelling the same cologne.

The door opens. The sound of soft steps enters, halting abruptly and preceding a weary sigh.

"I know I'm the last person you want to see," Dean says.

"You're right, you are," Shauna replies.

"He's my best friend."

"I know."

Why do Shauna and Dean sound irritated with each other? They like one another.

"Has anybody called his mom?" Shauna asks. "I don't know her number."

"I'll go by later," Dean says. "Though she won't answer the door. I'll leave a note."

"Thanks."

The door opens again. "Shauna Sandford?" a man asks.

"Yes?"

"I'm Detective Kerr. I understand you're Benjamin Thorton's wife?"

"*Wife?*" Dean says.

Shauna sighs. "I'm his girlfriend. I didn't think they'd let me see him if we weren't married."

"I see," replies Detective Kerr. "Either way, I'd like to speak with you. Privately."

5

A Few Days Ago

The green station wagon sits in the driveway, unmoved.

Inside the house, Mom's still dressed in yesterday's clothes, sitting in the recliner crocheting, her pale fingers with their bitten nails deftly working. She offers a confused smile when I walk in. "What're you doing home? Are you feeling okay? Did your class get canceled?"

I walk a lap around the living room and kitchen, noting her purse hung on the wall-mounted hook where it always is. Her shoes rest in line with others by the door. Her keys lay in the bowl atop the foyer table.

"Benny?" She notes my empty hands. "You didn't get the groceries did you?"

I backtrack, leaving the house and double-checking the station wagon. Am I sure it's in the same spot? I don't know. I place my hand on the hood, finding it warm. That's not saying much, as it's a hot day; the station wagon's bound to be warm.

Back in the house, Mom still sits in the recliner.

"Did you leave the house this morning?" I ask.

She flusters. "I tried. I promise, I tried."

I study her face, searching for falsehood, but don't see any.

"Benny?"

"I could have sworn I saw you on campus."

"What?" She laughs. "That's not possible."

I stare at her, wondering why she's still in yesterday's clothes. She's usually showered and changed by now.

Her head cocks. She scrutinizes my face. "You didn't sleep last night, did you?"

No, I didn't. But that doesn't mean I hallucinated seeing her.

She goes back to crocheting. "Was thinking pork chops for dinner. You going to be home?"

"I'm not sure." Silently, I watch her work. What am I thinking? Of course, she wasn't on campus. "Mom, I'm sor—"

"It's fine. See you later."

I hesitate, and then I leave her there to crochet whatever her latest project is. Probably another sweater that I'll never wear.

I've already missed class. I decide to kill some time at Dean's place. Plus I want to talk to him about Shauna. He knows I want to propose, but something is going on with her, though I'm not sure what.

A tiny cactus takes up a planter by his door. Dean's mom moved to Arizona a few months ago and she's constantly sending him care packages. Looks like the latest contained this spiny plant. What a good mom.

I raise my hand to knock on his door and pause, hearing voices—his and…Shauna's?

I don't knock. I use my key and let myself in, finding them on his two-seater couch, their heads fairly close together, softly talking.

"Shauna?"

She jerks away, coming to her feet. "Benny. Um, hi."

I study her blotchy face as Dean stands too. "Hey," he says.

I keep looking at Shauna's red cheeks and swollen eyes. "Have you been crying?"

"No, of course not." Quickly, she steps around the sofa, coming over to me. "Allergies."

Shauna doesn't have allergies.

"Don't you have class?" she asks.

"Don't *you*?"

Her throat clears. "It, um, got canceled." She takes my hand. Hers feels clammy.

Dean grabs his keys. "I was heading out. You two feel free to use my place." He sidesteps me, going through the door so quickly it rattles when he closes it.

Shauna kisses the back of my hand, forcing a smile. "How are you?"

"Fine."

"Good. That's good. We still on for lunch?"

She canceled lunch. I don't remind her of this, though. Instead, I say, "Sure."

"Great. Want to say noon at the taco truck?"

"Yeah, fine."

"Okay." Another fake smile as she comes up on her tiptoes to kiss my cheek. "See you later."

Then she skitters out, leaving me alone in Dean's place.

I trust Dean. I trust Shauna. These are the two things I remind myself even though uneasiness firmly takes root.

6

Childhood

The only person in this world who has ever truly loved me and who I love equally as much is my Pop Pop, Mom's dad.

He died one year ago today of congestive heart failure due to a bad cold that turned into pneumonia and went untreated for far too long. A visit to the emergency room became admittance to the hospital, then came ICU, and then death. It happened so quickly, I still don't quite understand. How can a cold make a person die? Mom says a lot of old people die that way.

He was seventy-six, yet I never thought of Pop Pop as old. Sure, he had thin hair, walked hunched over, and took forever to get up out of a chair, but still he seemed so young. He laughed all the time and played with me. He taught me how to throw a football. He let me hang out with him and all the other old people in his community, be it Bingo night or aerobics in the pool.

He lived in one of those communities reserved for old people. "Fifty-five and over" is what he called it. He had a modular home in line with tons of others. Pop Pop didn't have a lot of money. I think around thirty thousand dollars. That sounds like a lot to me, but Dad said it wasn't.

Pop Pop left the money to me, and Dad promptly took it. I don't know what he did with it. He certainly didn't put a new roof on the house, which we need. You'd think Mom would've cared he took the money her father left me, but she didn't. Or maybe she didn't care because Dad bought me a Nintendo, and he bought her a dozen roses, a bottle of wine, and a ring that turned her finger green.

But for one whole week, my parents got along. Dad snuggled with Mom. She cooked—actually cooked real food—every night. Dad played with me. Mom checked my homework. We were like Dean's family.

And then everything reverted with Dad yelling, Mom crying, and Dad drinking himself toward oblivion.

I think of that week a lot, wondering if Nintendo, roses, wine, and a ring that turns your finger green bring peace, shouldn't Dad give us presents more often?

~

MOM HAS BEEN INSISTING that Dean come over and stay the night. I don't know why. She suddenly seems so concerned about me: Have you brushed your teeth? Did you have a good day at school? Do you need help with your homework? How's Dean?

Maybe Mom had a come-to-Jesus, as Pop Pop would've

said, moment regarding motherhood. Either way, I don't want Dean coming. But then Mom calls Dean's Mom and I have no choice. Frankly, I'm surprised Dean's mom lets him stay over.

Mom spends the whole day cleaning our pathetic house in preparation for Dean's arrival. As we always do, we ride the bus home from school. Dean lives in the neighborhood next to ours, so our stop is the same. We pile out with all the other elementary and middle school kids, and my feet feel heavy as I trudge toward my home.

Most kids look forward to sleepovers. Not me. I never want anyone to be inside our house.

At my front door, I look at Dean. I hate that he's here. I'm sure he hates it, too, yet his expression seems normal. I'm about to tell him it's okay he can go home when the door opens.

Dressed in an apron, Mom grins. "Dean!"

Dean says, "Hi Mrs. Thorton."

"Come in! Come in!"

I feel sick as I step into our house. It smells like a combination of Pine-Sol, fresh baked cookies, and lasagna.

Mom bustles around us, taking our bookbags and ushering us toward the kitchen where a plate of homemade cookies awaits us. "Lasagna's in the oven!" Mom excitedly announces.

As she pours us both glasses of milk, we select a cookie and eat. I can't help but turn a slow circle, taking in our never-pristine home now free of dust, sparkling with polish, and tracks in the carpet from the vacuum. I look up to the corner where a spider web usually exists, finding it gone. Bummer, I liked that web.

"How does the house look?" Mom asks me, still grinning.

"Fine."

Her grin falters. "Fine?"

"It looks great," Dean quickly says.

Mom's grin comes back.

"Where's Dad?" I ask because he usually doesn't work on Friday afternoons. He's typically in the garage drinking beer and tinkering with a vintage Volkswagen—an investment, he told Mom.

It's probably what he bought with Pop Pop's money.

The front door opens and Dad walks in, still dressed in his work uniform from the factory where he drives a forklift. He comes to an abrupt stop, his gaze picking off the clean details of our typically unkempt house. "Oh, I see," he says, and I recognize the tone. It's the one that precedes the fighting. "You clean for Dean but not for your husband."

Mom's maniacal grin freezes in place. I guess it's too much to ask that both of them put on a façade for Dean's sake. Dad didn't get that memo.

"I made lasagna," she says through her frozen grin, teeth gritted and all.

He tosses keys onto the foyer table as he surveys Mom's apron and then the cookies on the plate. "Dean, you should come around more often," Dad says.

Her words come measured and ground out through the frozen grin. "Don't you have a car to fiddle with?"

Dad sneers. "Nah, think I'll stay here and eat some cookies and that lasagna. Because God knows when this little routine will happen again."

An eerie silence thickens the air. The calm before the storm.

Mom starts to cry.

With a sigh, I grab two more cookies and nod for Dean to follow me. We disappear down the hall as Dad's voice booms through the air.

In my immaculately clean room, we sit on the carpet, eating the cookies and looking anywhere but at each other. I don't know what to say. Dean sure as hell doesn't know how to react.

A crash echoes through the house followed by Mom sobbing. "I worked all day on that lasagna!"

"Should we...should we go help her?" Dean hesitantly asks.

"No." Every time I have tried to help, surprisingly she's the one who yells for me to butt out. I glance over to the window, streaked where she wiped in circles. "Want to get out of here?"

Dean nods.

His bookbag's out in the kitchen. We don't bother retrieving it, just climb out the window and walk the short distance to his house. His mom doesn't seem surprised to see us. I excuse myself to the bathroom, hoping Dean tells her what's going on back at my place. Hoping she'll let me stay indefinitely here. But when I emerge, she doesn't say anything to me, only hugs me and announces dinner will be ready in an hour.

That night I sleep on Dean's floor as I usually do. In the morning I wake to see Dean sitting on the edge of his bed staring at me with an expression I've never seen before —fear.

"What's wrong?" I ask, praying he won't tell me he doesn't want to be friends anymore. I wouldn't blame him after what he witnessed yesterday.

"Benny...do you...do you know that you sleepwalk?"

"No," I say, not entirely sure what sleepwalking means. "Why, what happened?"

7

Current Day

This is the most consecutive sleep I've had since I was a baby. If this coma can be described as sleep. It probably can. Because I drift, in blackness and back out. Sometimes I hear voices. Other times I don't. I feel people touching me. Then I'm alone.

As I am now. My best guess is that I've been here two full days now. I track the time by nurses coming in and out. I wish everyone would talk more. It's the only way I'm able to piece together the parts.

Sleepwalking.

That's what the raspy nurse said. Only three people know I sleepwalk—Mom, Dean, and Dean's mother. I never told Shauna. Luckily being Mom's caregiver always gave me an excuse not to sleep over with my girlfriend. One day I knew it would come up, but thus far I've managed to avoid it. Now Shauna must know. I mean, the nurses do, so I assume Shauna's heard.

Wait. Is *that* how I ended up on Shauna's roof?

The hospital door opens. "Good morning, Benny," a young and melodic female voice greets me. It's the same one from a couple of days ago. Still familiar, yet I can't place it. "Oh, I didn't see you there."

"That's okay," Shauna says, yawning and stretching.

"Why don't you get some coffee?" the young voice says. "Benny and I need privacy for the morning routine."

"Do I know you?" Shauna asks. "You look familiar."

"You've probably seen me around campus."

"Oh..." Shauna doesn't touch me or say goodbye. She simply leaves.

Did she stay the night? Why did Detective Kerr want to talk to her?

"Given that we know each other, I requested to not be assigned to you," the melodic voice says. "Unfortunately, we're short on staff, so here I am. I promise to respect your privacy."

Another person enters the room with a lazy, clunky-sounding tread.

The two of them begin a routine, familiar now of cleaning me and changing my diaper. I should be embarrassed, but I'm not. I'm grateful. It feels so good to be clean. Like I'm human and mobile. The clunky one doesn't speak, but the young one talks the whole time.

It's Thursday now. You've been here three days.

Oh, I thought two.

We had a pretty bad storm but it's beautiful out today. Let me open the blinds so you can feel the sun.

My body instantly warms and brightens. I must be by the window.

Your friend, Dean, was here again. You're very lucky to have such a great friend.

Yes, I am.

Let's comb your hair to the right today, hmmm?

Pop Pop combed what hair he had that way.

I'm not going to be here tomorrow, but if you wake up, I told them to call me.

The two of them continue moving around me. My body shifts as they wedge a pillow under my leg. They finish and leave. Shauna instantly reappears. My toes feel cold. Hopefully, she'll cover them.

She moves close to me, leaning over, blocking the warm sun from my face. I smell coffee and her halitosis.

"Can you feel this?" she asks, her voice barely audible.

Feel what? I don't feel anything.

She moves away, allowing the sun to once again warm me. "Do me a favor and wake the hell up."

∼

DAD?

I can't believe it. He's here. He's actually here. The last time I saw my father, I was almost eleven and he was sitting in a lawn chair in our garage drinking beer.

No, that's incorrect. He was in that lawn chair, his wrists flayed, covered in blood.

"Wow," he says. "You got big."

It's not Dad. It's Uncle Bobby, Dad's younger brother. And no duh I got big. That's what happens when you don't see someone for ten years.

He says, "I'm not surprised she drove both of you to this point."

What point?

"I know living with your mother hasn't been easy. Why didn't you call me? I'd have helped."

Whatever Uncle Bobby. I did call you. Several times after Dad killed himself. You barely had a minute to talk to me. I went from being a boy to the man of the house in one blink.

Uncle Bobby moves closer, finally sitting, but he doesn't touch me. I hear him breathing though. I smell the laundry detergent on his clothes.

"The doctor says you're stable. I don't know what that means. If you're stable, why are you hooked up to machines?"

Good question.

"I can't believe your mother hasn't come by to visit. I'm sorry her 'issues' keep her from being the mother she should be."

You dick. Your brother made her who she is. She tries her best.

"I suppose I should go drag her out of that house."

Don't touch her. Leave her alone.

The door opens. The sound of flip-flops enter, followed by a softer running shoe type tread. I smell Dean's cologne.

"Who are you?" Shauna asks.

"I'm Bobby, Benny's uncle."

"Oh…" Shauna crosses over and I imagine they're shaking hands. "I didn't know he had an uncle. I'm Shauna, Benny's girlfriend. This is Dean."

Shauna and Dean are together? I thought they were mad at each other.

"We've met," Dean says. "I was just a kid."

"I remember," Uncle Bobby says. "You got big too."

"How did you know about Benny?" Dean asks.

"A detective called me. Said he found my number in Benny's wallet."

After Dad died, I put Bobby's number in my wallet in case something happened to me and they needed a family member who could leave the house.

Shauna moves closer, touching my hand. "How's he doing today?"

"Doctor says stable," Uncle Bobby tells her.

"Oh, that's good. I'm actually on my way to an appointment. I wanted to stop in real quick and check on him."

"Have either of you talked to Benny's mom?" Uncle Bobby asks.

"I've called several times," Dean says. "I also knocked, but she didn't answer. No surprise, of course. I wrote a note and stuck it to their door."

"And I've never even met or talked to her, so of the two of us, she'd respond to Dean before me."

"What happened to your eye?" Uncle Bobby asks.

"Nothing of importance," Shauna says. "I tripped and fell."

"You're going to be late," Dean says. "We should go."

We? Where are they going?

"Nice to meet you," she says.

When they're gone and we're alone, Uncle Bobby says, "Jesus, you gave her that shiner, didn't you?" He chuckles, but there's no humor in it. "Apple doesn't fall far, does it there, Benny?"

8

A Few Days Ago

I sit in my second class of the morning, not listening to the instructor and instead staring at the clock. It's one of those manual ones that tick-tick-ticks its way through the day. I watch the second hand roughly click its way around the numbers and the little marks in between. The big hand sluggishly move to the next minute.

The professor raps his knuckles on the teacher's desk and I jump. "Please do not come to the next class without thoroughly outlining chapter ten. That'll be all. Have a day."

He always says that. Have a day. Not a great day, or lovely, or crappy. Just day.

"Benny," the professor says. "A moment please."

Crap.

After the class empties, I gather my supplies and go to stand at his desk. "Yes?" I say.

He sighs, heavy and deep. "You fell asleep. Again."

I did? That's impossible. I was wide awake staring at the clock. I turn to look at the clock, when I don't see one.

"We have talked through this," the professor says. "I know you have a lot going on at home, but you have to take care of yourself."

How does he know my home life?

"I am taking care of myself," I say.

The professor gathers his things. "I like you, Benny. Always have. It's not enough to come to class, you have to be present. It's part of your grade. Do we understand each other?"

"Yes, we understand each other."

"One more incident of sleeping and I will have to withdraw you from the course and issue an incomplete."

Panic sets in. "But I graduate soon."

"That should be plenty of motivation to stay awake." With that, the professor leaves and I survey the class walls again, indeed finding no clock.

So much for the caffeine pills I took, yet I take another.

My phone tells me it's several minutes past noon. Shauna's probably waiting for me at the taco truck. As I exit the class and walk the hall, I dial Dean.

One ring. Two. Three. It goes to voicemail.

He's ignoring me.

I leave a message, "I'd like to know what you two were doing this morning. I'm on my way to meet Shauna and something tells me she's not going to tell me."

I click off.

It doesn't take me long to walk the steps down to the first floor, out the door, and across campus to the taco truck where Shauna waits, sunglasses on, not smiling, watching me approach.

I come to stand in front of her. Her long brown hair's a

bit windblown and her cheeks flushed. She's never appeared more beautiful. It makes my heart hurt.

We don't greet each other, or touch. Last week we were laughing at two squirrels fighting over one peanut. We were happy. Or at least I thought we were.

I fell hard and fast for Shauna. We've been together for two years now. I'd have married her the night we met I was so far gone. But Shauna always gives the marriage topic a wide berth. She says it's because she's from a divorced family but I suspect it's not the whole truth.

Shauna leads me over to a picnic table under a live oak tree. We sit beside each other. She nibbles her bottom lip, studying the grain of wood on the table.

I try to be patient. In my head, my words sound calm, but when they come from my mouth, they snap out, "*What is going on?*"

She doesn't make eye contact with me, just keeps studying the wood grain. "This...this is really hard."

It's all I can do not to roll my eyes. I wish I felt gentle, but I don't. I'm edgy and getting angrier with each second. I take a breath and hold it.

"I'm..." She clears her throat. "I think it's best..."

She finally makes eye contact with me. I wish she'd take those stupid sunglasses off. I make a fist so that I don't yank them from her face.

"I think it's best if we break up."

My heart stops. The next words scrape from my throat. "What? Why?"

Shauna straightens up, suddenly seeming brave and bold. "We both graduate soon and this is not where I see my life. There have always been three people in this relationship. Me, you, and your mother. I love you, Benny. But it's time to pick. I'm not willing to share and bend my life for your mom. Not anymore." She stands. "It's me or her. Pick."

9

Childhood

I stand outside my parents' room, staring at the closed bedroom door because this is what Dean said I did during my sleepwalking episode. He said I left their house, walked through his neighborhood to mine, and used my key to let myself in. Then I stood and stared at my parents' door for nearly fifteen minutes.

It scares me that I don't remember this.

The door opens. With bloodshot eyes, Mom comes up short when she sees me. She doesn't ask me what I'm doing here or if I'm okay, she simply pushes past me and walks to the kitchen. A glance at their bed shows Dad still asleep, or more likely still passed out drunk.

I trail after Mom. Being Saturday, I don't have to go to school, so I sit at the kitchen island and ponder how I'm going to ask if she's ever seen me sleepwalking before.

Remnants of last night's lasagna stick to the floor,

counter, and wall where Dad threw the glass cookware that sits in a broken pile in the sink.

"Dean already gone?" she asks, not making eye contact.

She doesn't realize we didn't stay here last night. "Yes," I lie.

Mom gets an oatmeal pack, pours it into a bowl, adds water, then puts it in the microwave. Thank God the microwave was invented. We would starve otherwise.

She stands with her back to me, staring at the microwave as it counts down. Something's wrong. Despite whatever argument she might have had with Dad, she always, at minimum, makes small talk the next morning.

"Are you all right?" I ask.

She sniffs and wipes her nose with the back of her hand. But she doesn't answer me. Mom walks into the pantry and closes the door.

The microwave dings. I look at the pantry door, then back at the microwave. I wait, but Mom doesn't come out. With a sigh, I retrieve the now steaming oatmeal and then begin cleaning lasagna remnants from the kitchen, all the while listening to my mom cry.

~

UNLIKE MOST KIDS, I like school. I'm good at it. I enjoy learning and getting good grades. I keep to myself. I never cause problems. It's not that I'm popular because I'm not. But I know how to avoid being picked on. I guess if I had to thank my parents for anything, it's that. They've taught me how to skirt through life unseen.

School's my haven.

If I could go year-round I would; I love it that much.

Dean, on the other hand, hates school. He makes bad

grades. He wants so badly to be popular but it never quite works out. He also gets bullied for reasons he brings on himself.

Like now.

Our fifth-grade class is at recess. Everyone uses the new playground, but not me. I like using the old playground because it's always empty and sits at a distance from everyone else. I heard they might tear the old playground down. I hope not. Or if they do, wait until next year when I go to junior high.

But back to Dean. Sometimes he joins me at the old playground, but most days he hovers near the circle of popular kids, waiting to be invited in to toss a football, play tag, or hang out and talk.

Some days the popular kids ignore his presence. Other days they pick on him. Today's a pick-on-him day.

From a distance, I watch three popular boys surround Dean, roughly pushing him and taunting him with mean words. A teacher blows a whistle, shouting, "Hey, break it up!"

With sneaky sneers, the popular boys turn away from Dean, and after several solitary seconds, he trudges over to the old playground. He doesn't speak to me as he sits on a swing, his fingers twining around the rusted metal chain, and stares at the popular kids.

"Why do you keep trying with them?" I ask. *Aren't I a good enough friend?* It's what I want to ask, but don't. I'm afraid of the answer.

"Why don't you ever help me?" he asks.

"Help you what?"

"With them."

"What do you want me to do? I can't make them like you."

"I don't know, Benny. You're my best friend and yet I think you would sit here and watch if they ever decide to beat me up." Dean glances over at me. "Wouldn't you?"

He's correct, I would. Yet I say, "Of course I'd help."

"No, you wouldn't."

10

Current Day

I need to get up. I need to go to Mom. She's worried I haven't come home. Uncle Bobby's on his way there. He won't knock or ring the bell. He'll breach her line of security. He'll frighten her. He won't be gentle.

I need to get up.

I need to get up!

And then I do.

I sit straight up in bed. For a second, I don't move. I simply breathe, blink, and see. A machine beeps, but I'm no longer connected to it. They said I'm stable. I guess they removed the breathing tube and I didn't know it. The IV in my arm trails over and up to a bag of clear liquid. I grab that bag from its hook and swing my legs over the side of the mattress.

A cast covers my right leg, ankle to groin. A sling holds my left arm to my body. Carefully, I stand. The room sways, and I give myself a moment to acclimate. Then I gently put pressure on my cast, experiencing no pain.

Carrying the IV bag with me, I limp over to the door. It opens by itself, as if someone's coming in. But no one does, and I'm on the roof again, close to the edge. The wind kicks up. Overhead, dark clouds shift. Goosebumps prickle along my skin, alerting me that I'm not alone. My body feels stiff as I turn a slow circle, searching the stormy night.

A shadow emerges, growing closer. I focus hard on the face as it draws nearer, gradually becoming Shauna.

Then Dean.

Then Uncle Bobby.

Then Mom.

Then Dad.

Shauna. Dean. Uncle Bobby. Mom. Dad.

Shauna. Dean. Uncle Bobby. Mom. Dad.

Shauna.

Dean.

Uncle Bobby.

Mom.

Dad.

I jerk awake.

I try to open my eyes but they remain glued shut. I try to move any one of my muscles, but they stay firmly cemented in place. I try to speak, but the breathing tube prohibits it. I'm not well and walking, I'm back here in the bed, still in the coma, waking from a nightmare yet still trapped in the other.

11

A Few Days Ago

I'm still sitting at the picnic table. I don't know how long I've been here. Enough time for Shauna to leave. For the taco truck to close. For me to miss my afternoon class.

I'm frozen in time, replaying Shauna's words. Replaying every goddamn second of our two-year relationship.

We've been happy. She told me time and again my mother wasn't an issue, and believe me, I asked—or more continuously apologized.

I'm sorry I can't go to the concert; Mom needs me.

I'm sorry I can't stay over; Mom will have a meltdown.

I'm sorry I can't take you to the Taste of St. Augustine; Mom's having a hard day.

I'm sorry...

I'm sorry...

So why say anything different now? Why make me pick?

Shauna knows it's not that easy. I can't choose her over Mom. It would send my mother into a spiral she would never come back from.

I'm sorry...
I'm sorry...
I'm sorry...

Who am I kidding? No one would put up with that. I can't believe Shauna did for so long.

"Benny?"

I blink out of my trance, noticing the coffee cart girl. Only she's not dressed in an apron like I usually see her. She's wearing scrubs with a name tag affixed to her top that reads, BRITTA.

Well, at least now I know her name.

"Hi, Britta." It feels both weird and a relief to finally greet her with something other than, "Hey."

She smiles a little too widely at my use of her name. "What're you doing out here alone?"

"Just thinking." I stand and stretch my legs. "I need to get home."

"Okay, see you around."

I start to walk away and turn back. I'm not sure why I turn around. I'm not necessarily interested but she's always been so nice to me that my manners kick in. "I take it from your scrubs that you're studying medicine?"

Her wide smile brightens. "I sure am. In fact, I already work at the hospital. The coffee cart job gives me extra cash."

Manners done, I give a wave and walk off, calling Dean as I do. It shocks the hell out of me when he picks up.

"Hey," he cautiously answers.

"Shauna gave me an ultimatum. Her or Mom."

Silence.

"Did you know?" I ask.

"No, I...didn't. Wasn't expecting that."

"Well, then why was she at your place? I assumed she was talking that over with you."

Again, silence. His tension vibrates through the line.

"I promised her I wouldn't say anything," he says.

An odd numbness settles through my limbs. "Dean, what the hell man? Say anything about what?"

"You need to talk to Shauna. I'm not involved."

"The hell you aren't. I found my girlfriend at your place crying. Soon after, she gives me an ultimatum that she has never given me before. And you apparently know why."

"I said, you need to talk to Shauna." With that, he hangs up.

A yell erupts from me. I throw my phone at a tree. Then I stand in the middle of campus breathing angry, fiery breaths. I get more than my share of weird looks from passing students.

Thankfully, my phone didn't break. I dial Shauna. No big surprise, her voicemail picks up. I decide to lie. "Dean told me why you were at his place." I leave it at that and hang up.

At home, I slam the front door closed. I go straight to the garage and over to the extra refrigerator. I grab a beer and slam the whole thing. I grab another and drink it just as fast. The alcohol kicks in. My body sways. I take one more, hit the button to open the garage door, and go sit on a lawn chair as I drink the third.

Life father, like son.

That thought has me slamming the third beer.

The door leading into the house opens. Mom appears, still wearing yesterday's clothes. She gives the three empty cans a weary look that I ignore. Then she glances hesitantly at the outdoors bleeding its way through the open garage. I ignore that as well. Dealing with her phobias right now is at the bottom of my list.

"You want dinner?" she softly asks.

"I'm drinking my dinner." I get up and go to the refrigerator where I get three more beers, making my point.

"You...you should probably eat something."

"And you should probably take a shower." I pop the top and slam the fourth one glaring at her the whole time.

My mean comment doesn't seem to faze her. "I don't suppose you ever made it to the grocery for me?"

"Correct." I burp loud and long and annoyingly rude.

She takes the hint and leaves me alone.

That night when I finally stumble inside, I go straight to the freezer, select a frozen dinner featuring meatloaf, and toss it in the microwave.

In the living room, I eat it, staring down the hall at my mother's door.

It's been a long time since I tried the knob. I bet she still locks it. I want to scream, *Do you have any idea what I sacrifice for you?!*

Instead, I finish my dinner and pass out.

12

Childhood

My usually skinny mom is getting fat. I don't know why. I rarely see her eat. Instead, she's suddenly drinking wine from a box.

She used to pour the wine into a glass. Not anymore. Now she puts it in a big tumbler with a straw.

I watch her do just that as I make a peanut butter and jelly sandwich. I don't know why I ask the next question, perhaps it's the stupidity of childhood, but it comes out anyway.

"Are you and Dad alcoholics?" I ask.

Her pouring comes to an abrupt stop. Carefully, she places the wine box on the countertop and fits the top on the tumbler. With the straw in place, she takes a long, deep drink. I watch the blush-colored liquid enter the long, clear straw and disappear between her lips.

She swallows, holding the tumbler firmly in her hand.

Her question comes matter-of-factly. "Do alcoholics make their children food?"

My answer comes just as matter-of-factly. "You don't make me food. You microwave things."

Her jaw tightens. "I made cookies and lasagna when Dean came."

"Yeah, that one time," I say, not sure why I'm being so mouthy with her.

Her eyes narrow. A lot of weird seconds go by. Then she takes another long and deep drink. I finish making my sandwich and screw the lids back on the peanut butter and jelly. I should be scared, I guess, at her narrowed eyes and tight jaw, but I'm feeling more empowered. Though if this was Dad, I wouldn't be.

"When have I ever slurred my words or stumbled around this house?" she asks next, her tone still steely.

True, she's never done that. That's more Dad's thing.

"Because that's what alcoholics do," she continues and then takes another long drink. "You've never found me passed out, have you?"

"No." Again, that's Dad.

She takes yet another big drink. I watch her, noting an anger creeping in that reminds me of my father.

"Do you go without?" she asks next, her tone oddly still flat. "Do you have a roof over your head, a bed, bills paid, and food available?"

Hesitantly, I nod, no longer feeling empowerment. I wish I could take back my question.

Another drink, this one a sip. "Then how can you sit there like an entitled brat and judge me? The one you should be judging is your father."

I don't respond. I want out of here. Now.

"You want to see an alcoholic? I'll show you an alcoholic." She picks up the jelly jar and throws it at the wall. It shatters, spewing sticky clumps of grape.

Next, she grabs my sandwich and shoves it down the garbage disposal. The plastic peanut butter jar she hurls at me, and I duck, tucking in under the kitchen island. I'm about to run to my room when she appears with a jug of milk that she opens and dumps all over me.

"Is *this* what you wanted?" she yells. "You want an out of control alcoholic mother? Well, guess what, you got it!"

I try to crawl away but she stalks me out of the kitchen and through the living room. She's never once hit me, but for the first time in my life I am terrified of my mother.

The front door opens, and Dad walks in. Mom leaves me and with a scream, she runs at him. She smacks him across the face. It takes him a few seconds to register what happened. Then he punches her. She goes down hard.

I scramble away, running to my room. I close and lock the door, and I stand covered in milk and cry.

I'm glad Dad hit Mom.

~

I STAY AWAY from my home as much as possible. If there's something to do after school, I do it. If Dean doesn't invite me over, I invite myself. If I do have to go home, I go straight to my room and lock my door.

Today no one's home, though. It's paradise. I make microwave popcorn and sit in the recliner as I watch TV. I'm so engrossed in cartoons I don't hear the front door open. I don't see Mom go to the kitchen. I don't even notice when she stands in the doorway of the living room, drinking from her tumbler, and staring at me.

No, it's not until I get up to go to the bathroom that I catch sight of her.

My gaze goes directly to her black eye. It looks bad, but I still feel she deserved it.

She taps it with an index finger. "This is your fault."

I don't respond. She's got that odd, flat tone again. It scares me.

She takes one step toward me. I take one step back, my legs coming up against the recliner.

"You owe me an apology," she says.

"I-I'm sorry."

"That doesn't sound like you mean it." One more step and she's in my face. I wish I was older and taller, towering over her like Dad does.

"A better apology. Now." Her breath smells like wine. The sourness of it makes me wince.

"I'm sorry, Mom."

She sneers.

When did my mom become so mean?

Loudly, she slurps from the straw. The sound tunnels down my ears and snakes around my skull. My hands make fists. I've never punched anyone before. Mom might be the first.

Luckily, her phone rings and as she turns away to answer it, I run from the house.

There are several kinds of drunk people: happy ones, mean ones, sloppy ones... Unfortunately, neither of my parents is the happy version.

That night when I'm sure it's safe, I sneak back in. I find Dad passed out drunk in the garage slumped in the backseat of the Volkswagen, and I find Mom passed out drunk on the couch.

I used to wish my dad was dead. Now I wish they both were.

~

Mom's shrill scream wakes me. My first inclination is to see if she's okay—a few short days ago I would have—but now I don't care. I stay in bed, listening to Dad's voice, footsteps hurrying around, and another shriek from Mom.

Dad yells, "Benny, I'm taking your mom to the hospital!"

I come out of my room.

Mom sits on the couch, looking hung over, holding a blood soaked towel to the side of her head. On the coffee table rests a small porcelain steak knife, covered in blood. The couch cushion has blood too.

"What happened?" I ask Dad.

"I don't know," he says, grabbing his keys.

"I'll tell you what happened, one of you did this to me." She takes the towel away, revealing a long bloody line down her face.

"You did that to yourself, you drunk bitch, and you're trying to blame us." He yanks her up and drags her from the house.

After they're gone, I pick the knife up, feeling the slight weight of it in my hand. Pop Pop gave them this knife set, six in all. I've never used them, but I remember Pop Pop saying how very sharp they are.

I look at the blood on the couch.

Mom's crazy. One of us didn't cut her with this.

13

Current Day

I'm scared.
    Scared of being helpless in this bed.
    Scared of not waking up.
Scared of what happened on that roof.
Scared of Shauna. Dean. Uncle Bobby. And, for the first in a long time, I'm scared of my mother.

Uncle Bobby's here again. He returned some time ago, yet he hasn't said one single word. I imagine he's sitting beside my bed, staring at me.

Why isn't he speaking?

Uncle Bobby's not a quiet man. It's one of the things that has always annoyed my mother. Uncle Bobby always has so much, too much, to say about everything. He likes showing, or rather acting as if he knows the ins and outs of the world.

When I was eight he took me on a camping trip. After I helped Uncle Bobby set up the tent, we started a fire, and as we roasted hot dogs, I listened to him drone on and on. I pretended to be interested, but my God was I bored.

When he paused for a breath, I boldly copied Mom's words, repeating in a snarky voice, "You're such a *big* talker."

Uncle Bobby got silent. Real silent.

Not me, I kept going. "Mom says everyone knows you're a fake. No one's interested in what you have to say. People only tolerate you."

Uncle Bobby's eyes narrowed. "You finished?"

I shrugged.

"You're a little shit and your mom's a bitch. I want you to know that I'd rather be anywhere but here. I'm only doing this because your grandfather's paying me to while your parents work out problems you and I both know they won't work out."

He wasn't wrong. When I got home, things weren't different.

14

A Few Days Ago

My banging head wakes me. Time stops as I stare at an unfamiliar ceiling. My body moves in slow motion as I sit up. My mind races through events. The last thing I remember, I was drinking beer in the garage. I ate, eyeing Mom's locked door, and then I passed out on the couch.

My eyes sweep the room. Why am I on Mom's bed?

Still in the clothes from two days ago, she doesn't make eye contact with me as she walks in. Her feet pause mid step. She remains a healthy distance from me as she says, "Are you awake?"

"Yes."

Nervously, her hands clasp and unclasp.

My gaze roams her body. "Are you okay?"

"I'm fine."

"Mom, what happened?"

"The usual. You were sleepwalking. You would not stop turning my knob. Eventually, you did. But when I opened the door, you were in the kitchen staring at the knives. You haven't done that in a very long time. I ducked into the garage, and that's where I stayed the night."

"Oh, Mom…" I stand up. "I'm so sorry."

She shrugs, seemingly indifferent.

Carefully, I go to her. She allows me to hug her, but she doesn't hug me back. "Mom, I'm sorry. You know I'd never hurt you, right? *Never*."

"You scared me, Benny."

"I know. I'm sorry." I kiss her head. "There were some things that happened with Shauna, and it set me off."

"Anything you want to talk through?"

I should not tell her. I absolutely should not. Unfortunately, the words tumble out. "She told me to pick: her or you."

Mom pulls away. She gives me a long study. I try to read her expression but none exists. It's the oddest look I've ever seen. Like her brain contains no matter. "It's time you knew what really happened the night your father died."

15

Childhood

Dean got beat up at school today. I saw the whole thing and didn't help. He got suspended, along with the three boys who ganged up on him. I'm not sure why Dean got suspended when he was the one with all the cuts and bruises, but he did.

After school, I went to see him at his house. His mom answered the door, her face unreadable. When I asked to see Dean, she said he wasn't available.

I went again the next day and received the same response.

The next day, and the same response.

On the following day, Dean comes to the door. Aside from a tiny bruise on his jaw, he seems okay. I feel so relieved to see him, that I smile big. "Hey," I say.

"Hey," he murmurs.

I try to go into his house, but he blocks me. My smile slides away. "What's wrong?"

"I'm...I'm mad at you. You're my best friend. You're supposed to help me in a fight."

That's not fair. Just because he got into a fight doesn't automatically mean I have to as well. I like school. I'd be so upset if I got suspended. It would be the worst thing ever for me. There's enough fighting at my house. I don't need it at school or with Dean.

I don't say any of that; I simply turn around and leave. I don't know what this means, but Dean's the only friend I have. It hurts that he's mad at me.

It's been a month since everything that happened with Mom and the knife. She came home with six stitches, went straight to the kitchen, and poured her recently bought box of wine down the sink. She hasn't had a drink since.

Instead, she puts all her energy toward cleaning, and Dad pretty much leaves her alone. They seem to be getting along, or rather tolerating each other. I've seen them talking quietly a few times now, like they're sharing secrets, only to stop when I walk into the room.

Now, I find Mom using a toothbrush and bleach to meticulously scrub the grout in the kitchen. I know it's not there, but my gaze still tracks up to the corner the spider web used to occupy.

I leave her alone and go to my recently cleaned room. As I do homework, the house gradually begins to smell like cooking—yet another thing Mom now does. No more microwave meals.

Dad arrives home from work. I listen to their voices echo through the house in a normal tone, no arguing.

Sometime later, Mom knocks on my door. "Dinner," she says, her voice flat.

Dad's already at the kitchen table, serving himself baked meatballs with steamed broccoli and macaroni and cheese. My eyes widen at the homemade meal.

Mom puts a can of beer in front of him. We're quiet as we eat. When Dean's family has dinner, they chat the whole time. I search my brain for something to say and come up with nothing. Plus, I don't want to jinx whatever delicate balance they have going on now.

Halfway through the meal, Dad says, "Benny, do you know what sleepwalking is?"

Oh no. "Yes."

He and Mom exchange an uncomfortable glance. "We've caught you several times over the past few weeks in the kitchen going through the knives."

The meat in my stomach turns hard and heavy. It nauseates me. I look at the scar on my mother's face where six stitches used to be. *Shit, I did that?*

Dad says, "Until we know what we're going to do, we've decided to lock you in your room at night."

"What?" I feel sick.

"I bought a padlock today. After dinner, I'm going to put it on the outside of your door. I'm sorry. We can't risk you harming yourself or one of us." He goes back to eating like he didn't drop a bomb on me.

I don't go back to eating. I think I'm going to throw up. "May I be excused?"

Dad nods. Mom stares as I walk away.

True to his word, Dad installs a lock on the outside of my door. That night I listen to him fasten it shut and when he turns the key, the clunk of it thunders through my brain.

∽

Mom's acting strange.

Her recent cleaning trend has morphed into a daily, if not hourly task. She also counts a lot now. She counts how many times she washes a pot; the items she places in the washing machine; and the strokes her toothbrush hits each tooth. She also circles the house, double-checking lights and doors. She arranges and rearranges the Tupperware. She bites her nails. And she won't leave the house, not even to check the mail.

Dad says it's my fault. He says I scared her so bad with the knife incident that it caused her to develop something called OCD, which didn't upset Dad. If anything, he encouraged it. "Don't forget to get around the toilets," he said, and Mom meticulously scrubbed that area too.

He must be right that it's my fault because she barely looks at me or talks to me anymore. I sort of wish she'd drink wine and be mean again. At least then, I got some attention from her.

Because she won't leave the house, a man comes here to talk to her. He smells like bologna, has no hair, and wears a suit that swishes when he walks. The morning before he arrives, Dad takes the lock off my door, patches the holes, and repaints. Dad tells me to wear nice clothes and as he scrutinizes my appearance he says, "The man from the state might want to talk to you. Do not tell him we lock you in your room each night. You know it's for your own good. You cut your mother. She's this way because of you. He'll arrest you and put you in juvenile detention if he finds out. Do you understand what I'm saying?"

I'm barely able to nod. *Juvenile detention?*

The man in the suit sits with Mom for over an hour. He talks about the word agoraphobia. He also speaks to me. I don't discuss my sleepwalking, the knife, or the lock. I must do good because he doesn't arrest me.

When he leaves, Dad puts the lock back on my door.

A week later, Mom receives a diagnosis of OCD and also agoraphobia, both anxiety disorders. She now gets a check from the state of Florida. A check Dad takes.

I've been researching anxiety disorders. Did you know sleepwalking's considered one?

Well, go figure.

I wish I could talk to the man in the suit about my nightly episodes. But I don't want to go to juvenile detention, so I keep it to myself.

16

Current Day

Once upon a time my mother was a good mom. When I was really little she did things like play with me outside, volunteered at my school, and even made my clothes. She laughed and smiled a lot. At least around me, she did. She gave my father another version of her, or rather he brought that version out.

I have spent many a waking hour picking apart years gone by trying to figure out their dysfunctional relationship. But I continually see things from a boy's point of view. Perhaps because I was there in the thick of it. I'm forever frozen in time as that boy who wanted any other parents but them.

The door to my hospital room opens. The smell of fast food drifts over me. It makes my mouth water. I'd give anything to eat real food again.

"Hi, Benny," the melodic voice says. "Don't mind me.

Thought I'd hang out and enjoy my dinner."

It's Britta, the girl from the coffee cart. I knew she sounded familiar.

Wrappers crinkle. Chewing sounds fill the otherwise quiet room. I imagine she's sitting, maybe with her feet kicked up, peering out the window as she enjoys fried chicken—because that's what it smells like. I wonder if it's KFC or Popeyes. Both sound great.

She says, "So much about you makes sense now. I can't imagine dealing with what you do. It makes me like you even more. I'm not one to gossip, but everyone says Shauna and Dean are fooling around behind your back. Some think that's why you jumped. Others say you and Shauna were fighting and she pushed you. Personally, I think the sleepwalking thing is a bunch of bunk."

I try to stay alert because I want to continue hearing her speak, but darkness pulls me toward delicious oblivion.

∼

BRIGHT LIGHT suddenly wakes me as a doctor pushes up my eyelids and checks my pupils.

"What are you looking for when you do that?" Uncle Bobby asks.

The doctor says, "Checking for brain death. If the pupil constricts, the brain is okay."

The bright light goes out.

"Why's he still on a ventilator if he's stable?"

"One more day, then we'll see how he does breathing on his own."

"And if he doesn't breathe on his own?"

"Back on the ventilator." With that, the doctor leaves.

Uncle Bobby says, "Do yourself a favor and die."

17

A Few Days Ago

It's time you knew what really happened the night your father died.

My whole body shakes as I shower. I don't want to believe what Mom told me. Yet if I'm being honest, I've always suspected.

Out in my room, the phone rings. It's Shauna's ring. Quickly, I dry off and race to answer it, but she's already hung up. I redial her. It goes to voicemail. I don't leave a message.

With a towel wrapped around my waist, I stare at myself in the mirror affixed to my dresser. I barely recognize the person staring back.

I make myself get dressed. I need to talk to Mom about Dad.

I step from my room into...silence. "Mom?"

A glance into her room shows her stretched out on the bed, sleeping. So peaceful. So trusting.

Quietly I pace over. From the edge, I take a fleece throw and gently place it over her body. She smells bad. I hope this no-bath thing isn't some new phobia she's developing.

I press a kiss to her forehead and I simply stand and stare down at her.

So fragile.

I want to hate her, but I can't.

∼

As I drive to campus, I dial Dean. His voicemail picks up.

"A lot is going on," I say. "More than you know. I need my best friend."

I park in front of the education building and pace the hall outside of Shauna's morning class that gets out in twenty minutes. Through the glass panel of the classroom door, I watch her slump in her desk, her head propped in one hand. She must feel my stare because she glances up, her face pasty and pale. She used to flush when she caught sight of me.

Carefully, she slides from her desk, crossing over and coming through the door. Up close like this, her pasty face glistens with sweat.

All thoughts of things I want to say grind to a halt, replaced with concern. "Are you sick?" I ask.

With a swallow, she shakes her head, then bolts down the hall, disappearing into the bathroom. I'm about to go after her when Dean rounds the corner, his phone to his ear, coming to an abrupt halt. We study each other from opposite ends of the corridor. Neither of us move.

Then with a deep breath, he slowly walks to me. "I was

listening to your message," he says, glancing at the classroom door.

"What are you doing here?" I ask.

"Crossing through the air conditioning." He puts his phone away.

The bathroom door opens. Shauna reappears. She freezes, looking at me, then Dean, then back to me. I think she's going to say something, to do something, but instead she dry heaves and runs back into the bathroom.

My gaze fixes on Dean, daring him to lie. "What the hell is going on between you and Shauna?"

"Nothing."

"The hell it isn't."

With a shake of his head, Dean turns away. "I'm not doing this. Wait for Shauna and make her talk."

For twenty minutes I stand in the hall staring at the women's bathroom door, willing Shauna to come out. But she doesn't. Eventually, classes let out. The halls fill. Girls file through the bathroom door. Shauna never makes an appearance.

Fine, whatever. She wants to avoid me? More power to her. It only cements my decision. I dial her phone. "I'm outside the bathroom waiting on you. It's very immature to stay in there. I wanted to have this conversation face to face, but with the way you're acting, I guess I'm officially going to be immature as well. Shame on you for making me pick. However, I have chosen. I cannot leave my mother. Have a good life, I guess."

I go through my classes, barely registering anything. At the coffee cart, I see Britta, who hands me my usual Red Eye.

"Thank you, Britta." This brings a blush to her cheeks and causes me to pause.

Britta looks pretty today.

I'm not sure if it's the blush crawling up her face, or my girlfriend—rather ex now, I guess—giving me an ultimatum, or the relationship Shauna and Dean seem to suddenly have, or all the sacrifices I make for everybody, but I say, "Would you like to go out sometime?"

Surprise delights her eyes. "Yes! That would be great."

I'm pleased to feel a genuine smile crawl across my lips. "Okay."

We exchange numbers and I go on with my day.

That night at home, I stand in the garage staring at the spot where I found Dad all those years ago.

Mom's wrong.

I did not kill my father. I found him when I was sleepwalking. I carried the knife back to my bed. I know I did. Mom told me I did.

So why is she changing her story now?

Don't ever trust your mother. There's not a damn thing wrong with her. Watch your back. And if I ever turn up dead, you'll know who did it.

My phone lights up with Dean's number.

"What?" I say.

"I can't do this anymore. Shauna's pregnant. You two need to talk."

18

Childhood

It's been a month since I talked to Dean. At school he avoids me. On the bus to and from school, he no longer sits up front with me. He sits in the back on the outskirts of the popular kids. Every few days I call his house, but I end up talking to his mom because Dean's always doing homework, or gone somewhere, or in the bathroom, or a million other excuses.

His mom is nice, but I miss Dean. "Give him time," his mom says.

If I had good and loving parents, I'd ask them how to be friends with Dean again. But I'm not asking my parents anything.

So here I am sitting on the old swings, staring at Dean across the playground. He's been invited into the popular circle today, yet he appears more miserable than happy.

Probably because despite being invited in, no one talks to him.

I'm ready to climb from my swing when Dean walks away from the popular group and straight over to me. I barely breathe. What does this mean?

He stops a hesitant few steps away, looking at the ground and not me. "Hey," he says.

"Hey," I say back, trying not to show how excited I am that he's standing in front of me. "You've made some new friends, huh?"

Still looking at the ground, he shrugs.

"Why are you over here?" I ask.

Dean finally makes eye contact. "Because this morning I walked into the bathroom and saw Old Man Juke fixing a sink again..."

We bust out laughing.

Old Man Juke is the school janitor. Six months ago he was fixing the sink in the boy's bathroom when Dean and I walked in. Dean got a hand-me-down phone for his birthday and though the school prohibits phones, he brought it anyway. He was about to take a picture of the butt crack when I snuck into the frame. I got so close to Old Man Juke, I saw his butt hair. Dean got the picture and Old Man Juke never knew.

Dean takes the swing beside me. He glances around to make sure no teachers are watching and then takes his phone from his jeans pocket. He pulls up the picture. In it, I'm making a face with Juke's hairy butt crack only inches away.

We bust out laughing again, and just like that, Dean stops trying to be popular and becomes my best friend again.

Mom's check from the state must be enough because Dad quit his job and now stays home every day. Most mornings when I leave for school I find him in the garage passed out from the previous night's drinking. Most afternoons when I get off the bus he's in different clothes back in the garage and several beers in. He put an air conditioner in and a TV too. He calls the stupid garage his "man cave." It's a ridiculous name.

On the weekends when I don't go to school, I see what goes on during those hours I'm usually gone. Dad roams the house, following Mom, picking on her. She never responds and he eventually gets bored and goes to the garage.

I suppose the one positive thing to come of Mom's phobias is that Dad no longer yells at her during the night, she no longer cries, and I manage to sleep some.

Today is Saturday. When I hear my door unlock, I come from my room determined that Mom will talk to me today because she still barely acknowledges my existence. I see her wrapped in her robe walking down the hall away from my door.

"Thank you," I say.

She pauses, glancing back.

"For unlocking my door."

She nods, continuing on.

Dad's gone from their bedroom. I'm sure he's in his "man cave." He's rarely far.

In the kitchen, Mom makes coffee, ignoring me as I pour cereal. She keeps ignoring me as she drinks her coffee, staring out the window at our driveway very much in zombie mode. I don't recall the last time I saw her smile and

I definitely can't recall the last time she laughed. Hell, I barely hear her voice anymore.

"You look pretty," I tell her, not meaning it at all. She looks horrible.

The compliment doesn't even faze her.

I eat my cereal, watching her stand at the window, wishing I knew what to say, what to do.

With my cereal finished, I wash my bowl and go to the garage. Why I go to the garage I can't say. Maybe in hopes Dad's gone. But he's not. He's sitting on his lawn chair, drinking beer, and watching a fishing show.

"What are you doing, boy?" Dad drunkenly slurs.

Hell if I know what I'm doing.

He waves me over.

I approach, standing a careful distance. This annoys him, and he grabs my arm and pulls me closer. He smells bitter. "Whatcha got going on today?" he asks.

I shrug, wishing it's a school day and I have somewhere to be.

Dad slurps some beer, eyeing me through glassy eyes. "Want some?"

I shrug again.

From the cooler beside him, he pops the top on a new beer and shoves it at me. I don't want to drink this but I do. It tastes yucky.

"All of it," he says.

"I don't like it." I hand it back.

He shoves the can at my chest. "I said, all of it. Now."

He's still gripping my arm, and it hurts. I want to tell him that. I want to tug my arm from his grasp, but instead, I drink the whole beer, burping loudly after. Dad laughs, finally letting me go.

He crushes my can, gets another, and thankfully he doesn't shove it at me.

My head feels woozy.

He says, "Don't ever trust your mother. There's not a damn thing wrong with her. Watch your back. And if I ever turn up dead, you'll know who did it."

With that, he goes back to watching the fishing show and I stumble inside the house. I barely make it to the bathroom before I throw up. Mom appears, getting a cold washcloth and holding it against my head. It feels so good to have her near me.

After, she sits on the bathroom floor and I lay my head in her lap as she strokes my hair.

"I didn't want to drink it," I tell her.

"I know." She trails the washcloth along my face and I love it. I love that she's taking care of me. I love that she's being a mom.

"I hate him," I tell her.

"I hate him too," she admits.

My eyes close as she begins stroking her fingers through my hair. "I'm sorry," I say. "I never meant to hurt you with that knife."

"I know."

"You do?"

"Your father has turned the two of us into a dysfunctional mess."

"I wish he was dead," I boldly say.

For a very long moment, she doesn't respond, just keeps stroking my hair. Then in a voice so low I strain to hear her say, "Me, too, Benny. Me, too."

∼

Before, Then, Now 71

NO SCREAM WAKES ME. Yet my eyes fly open, my pulse pounds, and my breaths come heavy with panic. It's like a scream occurred, silent to the world, only blaring to me.

I sit straight up in bed.

My fingers clench something and I strain to see. But with the blinds shut tight and the curtains closed, I barely make out a detail. My hand stretches wide, releasing the object in my grip. I turn on my bedside light, squinting against the glow.

My eyes burn with the sleep I still need. It takes me a second to acclimate. That's when I see the porcelain steak knife nestled in my comforter, streaked in blood.

I leap from bed.

I can't get across the room fast enough. I'm prepared to bang on my door and yell, but when I try the knob, it opens. The lock's already been released. Or maybe it was never secured.

No, it's gone. There's putty in the drilled holes and fresh paint like when the suited man came here to talk to Mom.

The grandfather clock that used to belong to Pop Pop softly chimes. I stand frozen, counting the hours.

One.

Two.

Three.

It's three in the morning.

My bare feet move, seemingly on their own, stepping over the threshold. I walk the short distance to my parents' room, trying the knob and finding it locked. Perhaps that's what they've decided to do now—lock themselves in versus securing me.

I'm about to call out when the hairs on my arms stand up. I slowly walk down the hall, moving through the living room, and then the kitchen, finding both dimly lit, clean, and empty.

My pulse picks up pace as I backtrack, going toward the garage. I open the door, then stand, surveying the outlines of the Volkswagen, the extra fridge, the TV, the shelves packed with supplies, my bicycle, and various other things barely illuminated by a dim and flickering street light that filters in through the windows of the garage door.

I flip on the overhead light, and that's when I see Dad, slumped in the lawn chair, surrounded by crushed beer cans, his wrists slit and the cement floor beneath him saturated with blood.

My mouth opens. I scream.

∼

MOM CREMATES Dad's body and throws the ashes in the garbage.

Suicide. That's what they say Dad did. He slit his wrists. I never imagined that fate for my father. Frankly, Mom strikes me as more the type to have done such a thing.

It's been six months now. Mom's not any happier. The lock remains gone from my door. Instead, she secures her room every night in case I wander. I'm not sure which is the better option, but I trust Mom knows what she's doing.

I still don't sleep. I'm too scared to. When I sleep I have nightmares that I killed Dad.

That Mom did.

That I did.

That Mom did.

That I did...

19

Current Day

Leaning over my face, Shauna's halitosis isn't so bad today. She grasps the tube running down my throat. It shifts slightly, uncomfortably so.

"What are you doing?" Dean asks.

"Straightening the tube. It seemed crooked. Didn't it?"

Dean says, "You shouldn't touch it. You don't know what you're doing."

"Fine, whatever," Shauna says, and I hear her moving away.

"How are you feeling?" Dean asks.

"Fine, I guess."

"Any regrets?"

"Not a one," she says. "Thank you for going with me."

"I told you I would."

A beat or two ticks by.

"It was a boy," Shauna quietly tells him.

Wait, what?

Dean says, "It's for the best, given everything. For what it's worth, I am sorry that I told him."

"I know. We've moved beyond that. Let's not go back."

"Fair enough."

Another beat or two.

"You're a good friend," Shauna says.

"As are you," he replies. "Not a lot of girlfriends would still be around."

"Honestly, I don't know why I am. Call it sick curiosity."

"I'll admit, I have that sickness too."

"At least the focus is off of us now."

"True."

The door opens. The raspy nurse says, "If you two could give us some privacy?"

They leave, their steps fading, to be replaced by grief that quite suddenly spreads through my body. Inside I weep for a baby I never knew.

∼

IT'S SO QUIET. I don't hear the click of the ventilator, only a faint beep every few seconds. I think I'm alone, but I'm not sure.

The scent of fried food fills my nostrils. Maybe Britta's here again. Or perhaps it's dinner time with everyone around me getting meals.

My mouth salivates. I swallow.

I swallow.

Wait...

My tongue moves freely, unrestricted from a ventilator. I'm breathing on my own. I concentrate hard on moving anything—a finger, a toe, an eyelid—but nothing happens.

The doctor says, "Just because he's off the ventilator doesn't mean he'll wake up. He may even move, but that's an involuntary response. Much like our bodies twitching during sleep. It's only been a week, but you need to start thinking of long term care options."

"I don't have the money for that," Uncle Bobby says. "Shouldn't this be a state thing now?"

"Those are questions for Detective Kerr," the doctor says. "Here, though, we have a social worker who can help you secure a facility and funding."

I have never been the center of attention. That award has always belonged to my mother. Yet for the first time in my life, I am the center of everyone's attention. I don't like it at all. I wish I could give the honor to someone else.

I block them out, allowing my mind to dive deeply toward death. Because that's what I want now. I want to die. There's nothing for me if I live.

Darkness swirls, opening, welcoming me. I don't question where the light is. I don't deserve the light. I deserve the dark.

Yet the darkness doesn't want me. It shoves me away, catapulting me back. No! Please take me. *No*. "NO."

The voices in the room come to an abrupt stop.

My eyes open.

I am awake.

20

A Few Days Ago

The wind kicks up as I drive to Shauna's place. By the time I park and run inside, sprinkles have begun to fall, growing heavier with each moment.

In the hall, I bang on her door. She opens it in a rush, freezing when she sees me.

"You're pregnant?!"

Her gaze darts past me. "Shh."

"I will not. How dare you."

Shauna bristles. "How dare I what?"

"Go to Dean with this and not me."

She bristles. "You're not exactly easy to talk to."

"What the hell does that mean?"

"Honestly, Benny, what I wanted to say yesterday is pick me *and* the baby. But I didn't want to put that pressure on you. Otherwise... I plan on terminating the pregnancy."

"WHAT?!"

"But you picked your mother over me, proving what I always knew. I can't bring a baby into the warped relationship you have with her." She pushes past me, charging down the hall.

I follow.

Shauna swings open the stairwell door, charging up.

I go after her, grabbing her arm. She swings around, shocking the hell out of me when she throws a punch. I grip her fist midair. Her eyes widen. She kicks. I dodge the strike as she loses balance, toppling down a step, and face-planting into the iron handrail.

"Fuck!" she yells.

"Shauna!" I reach for her but she shoves me and runs the rest of the way to the roof.

I race after her.

The sprinkles have turned to full-on rain as I push through the roof access door, finding her standing staring out at the storm, not caring she's quickly getting soaked.

Carefully, I walk to her. "Please, Shauna, let's talk."

With her arms folded, she turns to me with a distant expression I have never seen before. Her eye is already swelling from the fall. She says, "Benny, I love you. I do. But it has never been easy."

My words come much more bitter than I intend them. "Well, I'm sorry I'm my mother's caregiver."

She takes a step toward me, her expression softening. "I love that you are so selfless, but it's too much. You're too complicated. You come with a lot of baggage. I thought I could get used to it, but I can't. I won't spend the rest of your mother's life helping you care for her. That's not what I want for myself, for our family. I want a life with *you,* not your mother. I've known for a while that hard decisions were coming, and here they are."

Shauna takes another step to me. The wind kicks her brown hair up and it whips my face. "I love you, but I'm done." Then with that, she walks past me and through the roof's door, leaving me alone in the rain.

Desperation rocks me. I cry hard. I sob for the life given me. For a life I could have if it weren't for my mom. For things I'm capable of. For the things I've done.

Truth is, Shauna and our unborn baby are better off without me. Even if I change my mind and pick her, it won't work. I don't trust myself.

Without hesitation, I dial the only person who truly knows every part of me and still stays with me.

My mother.

~

I don't know how long I stand here. Long enough for the night to settle in. For my clothes to become so wet and heavy they suction to my body. For the rain to stop. For the wind to continue.

My phone lights up with a text.

Dean: Shauna told me you're on the roof. you okay? I'm down in the parking lot. I can come up. I'm sorry.

I don't respond to Dean's text.

The door to the roof opens. My heart surges. But it's not Shauna who steps through. It's my mom. I can't believe it. "Mom?"

With a confidence I've never seen in her, she walks forward, coming to a stop in front of me. Tenderly, she takes my hand. I'm so shocked, I can't speak. Then I do. "You're out of the house. Mom, you're out of the house."

"For you, yes."

"Oh, Mom." I hug her hard. "I'm so sorry. I haven't been an easy child to raise. Your life hasn't been easy either."

Softly, she says, "You're going to be okay. You didn't mean to do it."

I pull back, searching her eyes. Her pale fingers with their bitten nails are wrapped around my forearms. "Do what? What did I do? Is this about Dad?"

Her soft expression gentles even more. She shakes her head.

A frown works its way through my face. Something in the recess of my mind tells me I should know what she's referring to, but I can't quite bring it to the surface.

"You can move on now," she says. "You're finally released. You don't have to worry about me anymore. Go, start your life with Shauna. I'll be fine where you left me. It's okay."

Her words mix and mingle in my skull, trying to fit together but still not snapping into place. Then suddenly she's no longer here. I turn a slow circle.

"Mom?" I quietly speak, knowing she won't answer.

I'm no longer on this roof. I'm ten again, standing in the garage, listening to my abusive father drunkenly snore. In my hand, I hold the sharp porcelain knife, now covered in blood.

Then I'm twenty-one, and it's a few days ago. I lie in bed, waiting for my alarm to go off, listening to the sound machine and smelling the lavender air freshener.

After a shower and applying Visine drops, I find Mom on the couch. She's in last night's clothes, eyes bloodshot and bulging, a maze of broken capillaries on her face, and bruising on her neck where I strangled her.

I leave her there, going to the kitchen where I start coffee and make eggs. I pretend to hear her voice, *Don't you look rested.*

I don't see her on campus.

Later, when I come back home I put her in the recliner and get her crochet needles. Like the horrible son I am, I accuse her of leaving the house. I pretend to hear her voice, *Was thinking pork chops for dinner.*

That night I get drunk on beer, hoping to forget what I've done. But she's still there when I finally stumble inside. I move her from the recliner to her bed, closing the door. From a selection of TV dinners, I choose meatloaf. I pass out on the couch in the exact location where I strangled her.

When I wake, I'm lying beside her in her bed. I remember our heated words, spoken two short nights ago before I killed her.

"Mom, you don't want to hear this, but I'm moving out. I want to start a life with Shauna. I'm planning on proposing."

Tears immediately spring to her eyes. The sight of them does nothing to detour my decision. Neither does the panic attack she launches into.

No, it isn't until she calms down and speaks, "It's time you knew what really happened the night your father died. Benny, you killed him and I covered it up."

"You're lying."

"No, I'm not."

"Yes, you are! I've given my whole life for you and you still want more. You're lying. You're manipulating me so I'll continue to stay here and never have a life of my own!"

I shove her, hard. Then my fingers wrap around her throat. All I see is the prison of this home stretching endlessly until the day she dies.

It happens quickly. So very quickly.

After, I stand in shock.

Then I break. I hold her. I stroke her hair. I cry. I promise her I will stay with her forever.

And over the next two days, I "play house" and pretend the whole thing never happened.

Back here on the roof, I gasp. No. *No!*

My phone lights up with a text.

Dean: Shauna's pissed I told you. I don't care. I'm still here in the parking lot. I'll stay as long as you need.

The phone drops from my hand. Numbly, my feet shuffle to the edge.

And then...I jump.

21

Current Day

I lay in my jail cell, staring at the underside of a striped stained mattress, listening to my roommate snore.

My lawyer wanted to plead insanity, but I refused. I wanted the maximum sentence. It's the least I deserve for what I've done.

It's been a year now of endless days, and nights, to think.

Uncle Bobby's the one who discovered Mom's body and told Detective Kerr, who determined I had strangled her after a heated argument about me starting a life of my own. It wasn't until I woke from the coma that I remembered the events on the roof: I wasn't sleepwalking and I wasn't pushed. No, I argued with Shauna, I had an imaginary conversation with Mom, I remembered what I had done to her, and then I jumped. If Dean hadn't been in the parking lot and saw me fall from the edge, I would have died. But he called 911, and here I am.

Uncle Bobby put the house on the market. I assume he pocketed the money, as I never heard otherwise. I don't care. Take the money and do whatever with it.

Shauna's moved on. She graduated and took a teaching job in South Florida. Nearly everyday I think of the life she terminated, wondering what my son would look like, sound like, smell like. After I play out the father-son fantasy I always come to the same conclusion—it's best he never knew me.

Dean still lives locally. He stops by once a month to visit me. I look forward to those visits. If things were reversed, I would do the same for him. I hope our friendship never dies.

Britta emails me now and then. She's sweet to do so. Her latest message said she met someone and is crazy about him. I'm happy for her.

I think a lot about Dad and Mom and my warped childhood. Like I'm ten again, I pretend I have different parents with a different life. I fantasize we're happy, we go on vacations, Mom is well, and I have the best dad in the world.

I might be awake right now, but oddly enough, I sleep well here in jail. A psychiatrist they make me see tells me I sleep now because my conscience is clear. I think it has more to do with the caffeine pills I no longer take.

My roommate chokes on a snore.

Using the pulley, I tug myself up to a sitting position. My wheelchair sits beside me, ready. I leave it there as I stare across and out the bars where a hallway stretches.

I know with one hundred percent clarity and certainty that I strangled my mother while I was awake. There was no sleepwalking to blame. Did I also kill my father? I don't know. Some nights I'm convinced it went down like Mom said—I killed him and she covered for me by claiming suicide. Other nights I think she did it and planted the knife on me, sowing that seed, just waiting for the time to nurture it—her way of keeping one last hold on me.

Before, when I was a little boy, I was trapped in a prison called home.

Then, when I grew older, I was trapped in a prison called obligation.

Now, I am a man, and I am trapped in a prison called life sentence.

But for the first time I feel free.

ABOUT THE AUTHOR

S. E. Green is the award-winning and best-selling author of young adult and adult fiction. She grew up in Tennessee where she dreaded all things reading and writing. She didn't even read her first book for enjoyment until she was twenty-five. After that, she was hooked! When she's not writing, she's usually traveling or hanging out with a rogue armadillo that frequents her coastal Florida backyard.

BOOKS BY S. E. GREEN

Ten Years Later

The Family

Sister Sister

Silence

Unseen

The Lady Next Door

The Strangler

The Suicide Killer

Monster

The Third Son

Vanquished

Mother May I

Printed in Dunstable, United Kingdom